For Arietta – A.G. & C.G.

For Rayven, Tom and Atlanta – T.K.

LADYBIRD BOOKS

UK | USA | Canada | Ireland | Australia
India | New Zealand | South Africa
Ladybird Books is part of the Penguin Random House group of companies
whose addresses can be found at global.penguinrandomhouse.com.
www.penguin.co.uk   www.puffin.co.uk   www.ladybird.co.uk

Penguin
Random House
UK

First published 2023
001

Written by Adam and Charlotte Guillain
Illustrated by Tom Knight
Text copyright © Adam and Charlotte Guillain, 2023
Illustrations copyright © Ladybird Books Ltd, 2023
The moral right of the authors has been asserted

Printed in China

The authorized representative in the EEA is Penguin Random House Ireland,
Morrison Chambers, 32 Nassau Street, Dublin D02 YH68

A CIP catalogue record for this book is available from the British Library
ISBN: 978–0–241–56346–5
All correspondence to:
Ladybird Books, Penguin Random House Children's
One Embassy Gardens, 8 Viaduct Gardens, London SW11 7BW

MIX
Paper from
responsible sources
FSC® C018179
FSC
www.fsc.org

5 FUNNY ANIMALS

Written by

Adam & Charlotte Guillain

Illustrated by

Tom Knight

It's time for Count and Seek –
would you like to come and play?

Let's count up all the animals
and see who's here today!

Four bears are in the kitchen and **one** more under the stairs.

How many altogether if you count up all the bears?

Five bears want an adventure,
but if **one** zooms into space,

how many little bears are left
to leap in cars and race?

Time to play!

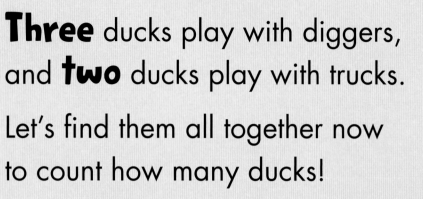

Three ducks play with diggers,
and **two** ducks play with trucks.

Let's find them all together now
to count how many ducks!

1 2 3

Five ducks are happy playing,
but if **two** ducks go inside,

how many ducks are left to splash
and wiggle down the slide?

Two frogs bounce on a trampoline,
while **three** bounce on a ball.

Let's count those frogs – I wonder,
can you spot them all?

FANCY DRESS

1

2

Five cheeky frogs together,
but if **three** play on the swings,
how many frogs are left
to put on sparkly fairy wings?

One cat puts on welly boots,
and **four** wear coats and hats.

Let's see if you can count them all
to find how many cats!

1

2

SPLISH!

Five cats are playing in the rain, but **four** have seen a mouse!

How many cats are left to sing and dance outside the house?

No goats are on their bicycles –
they all got into boats.

Quick! Count before they sail away
to find how many goats!

Five sailing goats land on the beach.
If all decide to stay,

how many of the goats enjoy
a seaside holiday?

The animals are hiding now.
They've gone – where can they be?

But maybe you can find them all . . .
How many can you see?

BALL
PIT

JUNGLE
FUN!

"You found us!" cheer the animals.

"Well done! Hip hip hooray!

We've all had fun
with numbers,

now it's time
for us to play!"

Look at how many ways the animals
had fun with numbers to make **five.**

How many ways
can you make
the number
five?